snap!

Mick Manning

Brita Granström

FRANCES LINCOLN CHILDREN'S BOOKS

Look!

A fly buzzing by...

Snap!

Fly is
in Frog's belly!

Frog gobbled
the fly that came
buzzing by...

Snap!

Frog is in Duckling's belly!

Duckling guzzled
the frog that gobbled
the fly that came
buzzing by...

Duckling is in Pike's belly!

Pike ate the duckling that guzzled the frog that gobbled the fly that came buzzing by...

Pike is in Fisherman's belly!

Fisherman caught the pike that ate the duckling that guzzled the frog that gobbled the fly that came buzzing by...

Here snores the bear that
swallowed the fisherman that
caught the pike that ate the duckling

For Quentin Blake

First published in Great Britain and in the USA in 2006
by Frances Lincoln Children's Books, 4 Torriano Mews,
Torriano Avenue, London NW5 2RZ

www.franceslincoln.com

Distributed in the USA by Publishers Group West

British Library Cataloguing in Publication Data available on request

ISBN 10: 1-84507-408-4
ISBN 13: 978-1-84507-408-1

Illustrated with collage, coloured pencil and black ink.

Printed in China
9 8 7 6 5 4 3 2 1